D1403800

© 1991 The Walt Disney Company

No portion of this book may be reproduced
without the written consent of The Walt Disney Company.

Produced by Kroha Associates, Inc.
Middletown, Connecticut.

Printed in the United States of America.

ISBN 1-56326-106-5

Daisy's Secret

By Ruth Lerner Perle

One afternoon, Minnie and Daisy were playing basketball when they saw their friend Lilly walking by. She looked very unhappy. Minnie waved. "Hi! Lilly!" she called. "What's wrong?"

"Oh, nothing," Lilly answered.

"But you look awfully upset!" Daisy said.

"Well...you see," she explained, "it's my birthday next week."

"Your birthday! Why that's nothing to be sad about!" Minnie exclaimed. "Birthdays are fun!"

"Not this year!" Lilly said. "I don't think anyone has remembered. Even you didn't know until I just told you."

Before the girls could say anything, Lilly turned and ran off.

"I wish we could do something to make Lilly smile," Minnie said.

"I'm not sure, but if we think very hard tonight, we might come up with something," said Daisy.

Then Minnie picked up her ball and the two girls started for home.

The next day, Daisy came running up to Minnie in the schoolyard.

"I've got it!" she shouted. "I know what we can do for Lilly. But I'll need your help."

"What is it?" Minnie wanted to know.

"I'll tell you, but promise to keep it a secret," Daisy whispered. "You can't tell anyone about my plan. It would spoil everything."

"I promise," Minnie said.

Daisy led Minnie to a corner and whispered her secret plan.

The first things Daisy needed for her secret plan were colored paper, markers, and envelopes, so Minnie and Daisy went off to the stationery store.

At the corner, the girls met Penny.

"Hi," Penny said. "Where are you two going?"

"Well," Daisy started, "we're going to the store."

"What for?" Penny asked.

"It's a secret," Minnie said.

"Oh, please tell me!" begged Penny, but the girls just waved good-bye and went on their way.

At the stationery store, Minnie helped Daisy find all the supplies they needed.

When they came to the check-out counter, Clarabelle was paying for some crayons.

"Hi, there!" Clarabelle called to them. "What's all that stuff for?"

"You'll find out soon enough!" Daisy said.

"It's Daisy's secret!" Minnie added.

Minnie and Daisy brought all their purchases to Daisy's house and got busy with the next step of the secret plan.

At school the next morning, Daisy and Minnie gave each of their friends an envelope with a card inside. Daisy and Minnie had cards, too.

Each card had a different, funny-looking word printed on it. In fact, they weren't words at all — just a bunch of letters that made no sense.

Penny's card
said: !ƎƧIᴚᴘᴚUƧ

Clarabelle's card
said: A ƎVAH

Minnie's card
said: VERY

Daisy's card
said: HAPPY BIRTHDAY,

and Lilly's card said: LILLY!

Everyone wanted to know what the cards were all about.

"Come to my house on Sunday at three o'clock," Daisy said with a twinkle in her eye. "That's when the mystery will be solved."

That's too long to wait! Clarabelle thought. *I want to know now!*

As soon as Minnie came home that afternoon, the telephone rang. It was Clarabelle.

"Hello, Minnie," she said in her sweetest voice. "What are you and Daisy up to?"

"I'm sorry, I can't tell," Minnie said.

"But you can tell *me!*" Clarabelle said. "I won't tell anyone else!"

"I'd like to, Clarabelle, but I can't," Minnie said. "It's Daisy's secret."

"You're no fun!" Clarabelle said as she hung up the phone.

As soon as Minnie put down the receiver, the phone rang again. This time it was Penny.

"What's going on?" she asked.

"I promised to keep it a secret," Minnie said.

"If you tell me the secret, I'll tell you one in return," Penny said.

"You'll find out what the secret is on Sunday," Minnie said.

Lilly called Minnie next. It was especially hard not to tell Lilly the secret because Minnie knew how happy it would make her.

But still, Minnie kept her promise to Daisy.

The next day, Minnie and Daisy went to the market together. Clarabelle and Lilly were there, too. They watched as Minnie and Daisy bought milk, cream, flour, eggs, sugar, and strawberries. "What will they do with all that?" Clarabelle wondered.

Daisy and Minnie brought the groceries home, then whipped
and stirred and mixed the ingredients, following a recipe in Daisy's
cookbook.

The next day was Sunday at last. Everyone came to Daisy's house promptly at three o'clock, carrying their cards with the funny letters on them.

"We can't wait!" Clarabelle said. "What's the big secret?"

"Yes, please tell us," Lilly said.

Then Daisy brought a giant strawberry shortcake to the table.

"That's a beautiful cake," Lilly said, "but how will that tell us what the secret is?"

"You all have the secret in your hands," Daisy said. She collected the cards and set them on the top of the cake. Then she took a hand mirror and held it up over the words.

"Now, everybody, please read the words you see in the mirror," Daisy said.

They all read together: SURPRISE! HAVE A VERY HAPPY BIRTHDAY, LILLY!

"*Lilly*! That's me!" shouted the birthday girl. "Oh my goodness! I've never had a surprise party before! This is the very best birthday I have ever, ever had!" Lilly smiled. "And it's all thanks to Daisy for thinking of this special celebration and to Minnie for making sure it would be a surprise."

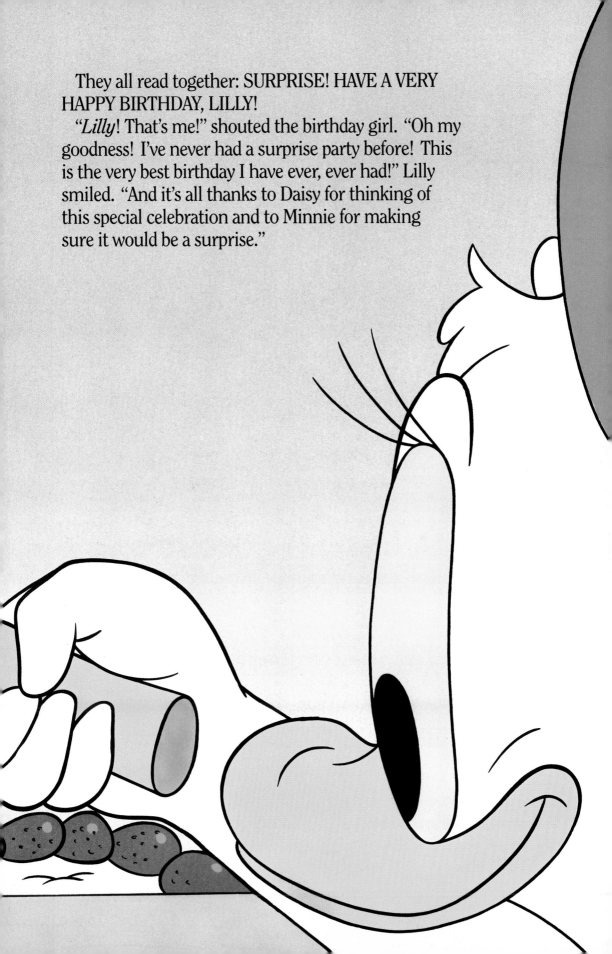

"It was a surprise for all of us! Now we know," Penny said.
"And I must admit, the suspense made it lots more fun,"
Clarabelle said.

Everyone sang *Happy Birthday* to Lilly, and then Daisy served slices of strawberry shortcake while Minnie poured the milk.

The girls had a wonderful afternoon playing games and telling stories — but Lilly had the best time of all.

Hold the facing page up to a mirror to read the surprise message yourself. And don't forget to send me the enclosed letter about a secret you had to keep. Please write to me and I promise to answer you soon.